CRUPI

BRANCH and the
Party Rescue

Scholastic Children's Books,
Euston House, 24 Eversholt Street,
London NW1 1DB, UK

A division of Scholastic Ltd
London ~ New York ~ Toronto ~ Sydney ~ Auckland
Mexico City ~ New Delhi ~ Hong Kong

First published in Australia by Bonnier Publishing, 2017, as two titles:
Branch and the Party Rescue
Satin & Chenille and the Makeover Disaster
This edition published in the UK by Scholastic Ltd, 2018

Written by Jaclyn Crupi

ISBN 978 1407 17145 6

Printed and bound in the UK by CPI (Group) Ltd, Croydon, Surrey

2 4 6 8 10 9 7 5 3 1

Papers used by Scholastic Children's Books are made from wood grown in
sustainable forests.

www.scholastic.co.uk

BRANCH and the Party Rescue

■SCHOLASTIC

Chapter 1

BANG! BANG! BANG!

Branch opens one eye. 'Ten more minutes,' he mutters and pulls his blanket over his head.

BANG! BANG! BANG! This time the knocking is louder.

Branch was hoping to have a lie-in. But now he's worrying about who is at

the door. Is it a Troll in danger? Does someone need his help? Branch leaps heroically out of bed. He runs into the lift and cranks the lever to take him to the top floor of his bunker.

Branch is the only Troll in Troll Village who lives in an underground bunker.

Since helping Queen Poppy save the Trolls from the Bergens, Branch has loosened up a little. But being a worrier is part of who Branch is. At heart, he truly believes being prepared and cautious is the best way to be.

His lift clunks to a stop at the top floor and Branch cracks open his front door.

There, before his 'GO AWAY' mat, is a little pink Troll with her hair magically curled into the shape of an umbrella. Pouring rain beats down around her.

'Hi, Poppy, is everything okay?' he asks, thinking only a disaster could bring Queen Poppy to his door on such a wet day.

'Good morning, Branch!' Poppy exclaims brightly. 'Everything is more than okay. It's perfect!' She throws her arms into the air. 'Isn't this the most beautiful day we've ever seen in Troll Village?'

Sometimes Poppy confuses Branch.

13

'But Poppy, it's rainy, grey and cold,' he says.

Now it's Poppy's turn to look confused.

'But every day is the most beautiful day, Branch,' Poppy says wide-eyed. She jumps up into a twirl, busting a move and shaking the rain from her tuft of bright pink hair.

Branch can't help but smile. 'You're right, Poppy, I need to try some positivity,' he says. And just like that the sun is shining again.

Poppy flicks out her hair umbrella and her hair springs back into its usual shape. She enters Branch's bunker.

As Branch is closing the door, he spots Guy Diamond dancing by.

'Guy Diamond, man, your glitter level is on its highest sparkle setting,' Branch laughs, shielding his eyes from the shiny glints radiating off Guy Diamond.

'You know it,' Guy Diamond sings before dancing off again.

Seeing Guy Diamond sparkling in the sunshine and Poppy bursting with enthusiasm makes Branch think that perhaps it is a beautiful day.

'Hey,' Poppy says, 'I have the best idea ever.' She looks at him seriously. 'Branch, I think you're ready to host your first rockin' party.'

'Whoa, Poppy, don't you think it's a little soon for that?' Branch asks nervously, 'I'm a party pooper, not a party trooper.'

'No you aren't, Branch. Everyone deserves to have fun – including you,' Poppy says, stepping closer. 'And there's nothing more fun than throwing a party and seeing all your friends have fun. You can do this.'

'I don't know,' Branch says. 'Parties are really not my thing. I'm more of a prepare-for-the-worst-case-scenario kind of Troll. I live in a bunker, remember? Besides, nobody will want to come to my party.'

'Of course they will,' Poppy replies confidently. 'And I've already started scrapbooking invitation ideas!'

'But I don't know anything about party planning,' Branch groans. 'Why don't you plan the party and I'll just come along with my first aid kit and fire extinguisher.'

'That's the old Branch,' Poppy says, hands on her hips. 'You need to embrace the *new* you. Let your true colours shine through.'

'Oh.' Branch is quiet for a moment. 'Well, maybe I could plan a fun party.'

Poppy cheers. 'Okay, well, I'll make the invitations but the rest is up to you.' In celebration, Poppy sings a happy song complete with fresh dance moves.

Branch is starting to feel a little bit excited about planning this party. 'Wow,' he says, clapping his hands. 'In that case I'd better start to get crazy.' Branch winks. 'Crazy prepared.'

Chapter 2

Branch is pacing in his bunker muttering to himself. Ever since Poppy left he's been in party-planning mode. Branch wants to throw a fun party and he's trying to think positively. But he can't help thinking there should be rules to keep everyone safe.

'Want a cupcake?'

Branch spins around and sees Biggie,

Mr Dinkles and Cooper standing inside his bunker. 'How did you get in here?' he asks, shocked.

'The door was open,' says Biggie.

'Oh.' Branch remembers that recently, with Poppy's help, he has reduced security in his bunker. He really is trying to be more positive and less cautious.

'Well I'm glad you're here guys,' Branch says with a smile. 'I need some advice about the party I'm planning at Glitter Falls.'

'Will there be cupcakes?' Biggie asks, looking intently at Branch.

'Ah, snacks – I hadn't thought about snacks,' Branch replies. 'I guess I can allow cupcakes. I don't see how they could pose any danger. In a marked food area. I'll appoint Satin and

Chenille as cupcake monitors as there could be a choking hazard with all the dancing.'

'How many disco balls will there be? Gotta love the disco ball vibe at a party,' Cooper says.

Branch is quiet for a minute as he thinks about this. 'Bright lights that shine in your eyes at random might be incredibly dangerous,' Branch says.

He is imagining a Troll being blinded by bright light and dancing right off Glitter Falls! 'I'm not sure we can have any disco balls.'

'What about glitter explosions?' Biggie asks.

'No, they are never safe,' Branch says firmly.

'Oh,' Biggie and Cooper say together, looking very glum. Even Mr Dinkles looks disappointed.

But Branch feels strongly about his decisions. He can't help but remember what happened that time the Trolls threw a big, loud, bright, crazy party ... it ended with the Bergen's Royal Chef capturing some of his friends. Rules and caution are the only way he can keep everyone safe.

'Well,' Cooper says, breaking the silence. 'I'm super excited to bust some new dance moves.' He shows off a few of them. They are wild and Biggie cheers loudly.

'Careful there, Cooper!' Branch shouts. 'You almost knocked over my wood pile.'

Cooper freezes. And then Branch continues. 'At my party I will allow dancing. But wildly swinging arms and legs are a huge hazard.' He thinks for a moment. 'I will allow dancing as long as every Troll agrees to stay in the dancing area, with arms firmly by their sides and not using their hair for swinging,' Branch says.

Cooper unfreezes. 'Just give us lots of cupcakes and blasting beats and we'll be happy,' he whoops.

'Blasting beats?' Branch shakes his head. 'Absolutely not. Loud noise is what got us into trouble last time. No, this party will have no loud noise and no bright lights.'

'No loud music and no lights, what kind of party is that?' Biggie asks, stealing a glance at Cooper.

'A safe one,' Branch replies.

'That doesn't sound like much fun,' Biggie mutters to Mr Dinkles. Biggie, Mr Dinkles and Cooper head to the bunker door. 'Um, I guess we'll see you later, Branch.'

Branch closes and locks his door, thinking through the next steps of his party plans. He sits down at his table. Okay, he has some rules, now he needs some fun party activities. A piñata maybe? He draws some different piñata designs. A Bergen-shaped one. A rainbow. A cloud. He has so many ideas! A piñata filled with sweets. His friends will love that!

But then he has a creeping thought.

How can he make a piñata safe? Someone could get hit with the stick. He's not sure how to fix that. He thinks of a different activity. Branch has always wanted to jump on a bouncy mushroom course. Perhaps he could make one. After all, he's good at building things. But then he thinks a bouncy mushroom course could be dangerous. What if someone bounced out?

The more he thinks about it, the more Branch's thoughts spiral out of control. It can be hard to plan for every possible thing that could go wrong.

He tries to be positive, but finds that he feels he needs some more rules. And they need to be written down.

When he finishes his list, he nails it to the door of his bunker and heads out to collect more firewood.

Branch's Ten-Rule Party Plan

1. Dancing allowed only in marked dancing zones*

2. No snacks allowed near the marked dancing zones*

3. Limit of 3 cupcakes per Troll

4. No hugs near the fruit drink stand

5. No up-high, hair-swinging dance moves allowed

6. No disco balls allowed

7. No light shows

8. No glitter explosions

9. DJ Suki to keep the beats at a low decibel

10. No scrapbooking allowed

*all Trolls to sign Dancing Zone Agreement before party

Chapter 3

The next day, Branch is walking through the fuzzy felt forest towards Troll Village. He spots Cooper, Biggie and Mr Dinkles just up ahead on the felt path and jogs up to speak to them. Just as he is about to call out to them he hears his name ...

'Branch's party sure has a lot of rules,' Cooper is saying.

'Yeah,' agrees Biggie. 'I heard he has written a Ten-Rule Party Plan.'

Branch frowns. News always travels fast in Troll Village.

Biggie, Cooper and Mr Dinkles wave at their other friends in a small clearing. Branch doesn't know what to do. So he stands behind a soft shrub.

It's obvious that the rest of Branch's friends have heard about his party rules, too.

'Nobody tells me how loudly I can lay down my beats,' DJ Suki is complaining. 'I'm an artist.'

'Nobody tells me what I can and can't do with my hair on the dance floor,' little Smidge says fiercely.

'Nobody tells me I can't be a disco ball or make glitter bursts,' Guy Diamond exclaims, shaking a huge glitter trail.

Biggie sits down. 'Nobody tells *me* how many cupcakes to eat,' he adds, gulping down a cupcake.

'And nobody tells me where I can and can't dance,' Cooper says as he busts a move. 'You can't control these four feet!'

'Come on you guys,' Poppy says. 'Branch is just trying to keep us safe.

But I don't love that I'm not allowed to scrapbook at all during the party either. I mean, how will I capture the moment without stickers and glue and fabric and glitter?'

Poppy gasps for breath, as if trying to regain her positive outlook. Then she grins. As Branch peeks over the shrub, he recognises that look. Poppy has some bedazzled item up her sleeve and she is about to use it.

'Hey, look! I made invitations and they're positively Troll-tastic,' Poppy says presenting the party invitation to her friends.

'Excellent,' coos Cooper, leaning in to take a better look.

It's a pop-up scene depicting the party. There are Trolls dancing everywhere. There are countless cupcakes. There are Trolls hugging. There are disco balls. There are glitter explosions. There's a bright light show. There are hair-swinging Trolls. It looks amazing!

'Nice invitation, Poppy, except that the party won't be like that at all,' Biggie says quietly. 'Branch's rules won't allow it.'

'Yeah, Branch's party is no party,' DJ Suki adds.

'We'd like to go,' Satin says.

Chenille adds, 'But it might be more fun not to go.'

The other Trolls each say that the party has too many rules and they don't want to go. They feel badly about letting down their friend Branch but they just can't have fun with so many rules.

Poppy's wild shock of pink hair droops. She looks a little worried.

'I'm going to find Branch,' she says. 'I know he can do this, but he needs my help.' At that moment, the Trolls' Hug Time watches blossom.

'Hug Time!' they all cheer and come together for a giant group hug.

Nobody has realized that Branch was on the other side of a shrub this whole time and has heard every word.

chapter 4

Branch is feeling blue even though he is looking more teal. He thought he was getting the hang of this positivity thing. Perhaps his rules were a bit too much. But 'safety first' has always been his approach. He did try to plan fun activities but his focus quickly became rules and safety. He's trying to change but it's not always easy.

When his friends have left the clearing, Branch leaves his spot behind the shrub and heads home. On the way, he bumps into Poppy.

'I showed the gang my invitation,' Poppy says. 'Everyone is really excited about the party.'

'You don't have to hide it from me,' Branch says glumly. 'I know nobody wants to come. I heard everything that everyone said.'

Poppy looks sad, but says nothing.

'Yesterday I thought I might be able to plan a fun party, but I just can't help thinking about all the things that might go wrong. I guess it takes the fun out of everything. I've done all this work and preparation for nothing. I even made cupcakes!' Branch says.

'Aw, you made cupcakes.' Poppy sounds impressed. 'You're a real trooper, Branch. I'm proud of you.'

'I shouldn't have bothered,' Branch says. 'It's true. I ruin everything, especially anything fun. I'm not a party trooper. I really am a party pooper.'

'No you're not, Branch,' Poppy says. She feels guilty. 'And I've let you down. My invitations didn't inspire our friends. I'm so sorry. I really made a mess of things.'

Branch is surprised. He is not used to seeing Poppy so upset. She's usually the positive one! It stirs something

44

inside him. It makes him want to be more positive.

'Can I see your invitation?' Branch asks.

Poppy smiles weakly and hands Branch an invitation. He looks at the scene in her diorama. Trolls dancing everywhere! So many cupcakes! Constant hugging! Glitter explosions! Bright lights! Just looking at the invitation makes him feel happy. It looks like a great party. And it does seem quite safe. Maybe he could make a few adjustments so the party is more about having fun than following safety rules.

'I've got to go, Poppy,' Branch says.
'I have an idea.'

Back in Troll Village, Guy Diamond is about to have his own idea.

'Even though Branch's party plan was full of rules, I'm so sad that we're not having a party anymore,' Biggie sobs.

'Who says we can't still have a party?' says DJ Suki.

'That's right,' says Guy Diamond. 'I'm going to throw the biggest, the loudest, the craziest party Troll Village has ever seen! The only rule will be there are no rules.'

'Super cool!' Satin and Chenille say.

'It will be the sparkliest glitter party EVER!' Guy Diamond continues. 'The shine will be blinding!' Guy Diamond can't help but make a glitter trail to show what he means. 'We'll invite Branch of course and show him how to relax and go with the flow. And then maybe he could plan our next party.'

Biggie bursts into a fit of happy tears.

ALL the Trolls want to go to THIS party. 'No rules' sounds like the perfect kind of Troll party. What could possibly go wrong?

Chapter 5

Guy Diamond's party by Glitter Falls is not going well and he is frantic. He kicked off the party by dancing up a huge wild, crazy glitter storm. It is more glitter than the Trolls have ever seen! Now the dance floor is sparkly and shiny and shimmery and bright and ... *slippery*.

Biggie was so excited about the party that he immediately started crying

happy tears. A lot of happy tears. It turns out that glitter mixed with tears makes for a crazy slippery dance surface.

Trolls are slipping and sliding across the dance floor. And not in a good way. Things are getting more and more out of control. Guy Diamond is scared someone might get hurt. He may know how to kick off the fun but he has never thought about what to do if things were to go wrong. It doesn't even cross his mind. He just wants to make sure everyone has fun.

There is only one Troll who knows what to do in an emergency. And he decided to stay at home.

'Satin, Chenille, go get Branch. We're going to need his help,' Guy Diamond shouts in his autotune voice.

Satin and Chenille swing through Troll Village to Branch's bunker faster than they ever have before.

'I think we broke our speed hair altitude record,' Satin says as the twins burst inside.

Branch is removing netting from around the bouncy mushroom course he has been building. He feels happy with his work.

'Branch, come quick,' Chenille shouts. 'The party needs your help.'

Seeing the worried looks on their faces, Branch drops everything and follows the twins to Glitter Falls. They meet Poppy on the way and she joins them.

'Quickly!' Satin says. 'Before someone gets hurt.'

When Branch, Poppy and the twins arrive, Guy Diamond's party is in chaos. Trolls are skidding and tripping all over the place and glitter is flying through the air like a sparkling haze. Some Trolls look like they are having fun but it's completely out of control.

Branch watches as Smidge slides for what seems like miles and falls face first into some colourful wildflowers.

Poppy jumps out of the way just in time when Cooper slips by, each of his four legs kicking out in different directions. He slams into Biggie bumping Mr Dinkles right out of his arms and into the air as he falls backwards. Branch catches Mr Dinkles just before he hits the ground.

'That was close,' Branch says, looking on. 'We got here just in time.'

'This party is crazy,' Poppy says. 'And not in a good way.'

Branch nods, looking around. The floor is getting more soaked in tears and even more slippery than before. Fuzzbert is the latest victim, sliding out of sight.

'HELP!' screams Guy Diamond as he glides bottom first on a glitter burst.

Branch and Poppy share a knowing look. Branch knows what to do. And Poppy knows it. Branch to the rescue!

Chapter 6

Branch's years of training for disaster kick in and he goes into action mode.

He yells instructions to Poppy, Guy Diamond and Biggie. 'Go get my party treats and activities. This party is going to need some fun!' Branch ignores their surprised faces. 'I'll clean up this mess.'

Branch extends his blue hair into a broom and sweeps the floor clear of

glitter and tears. The Trolls still on the dance floor are skillfully caught by Branch's hair and safely deposited to the side. Branch whips his hair back and forth a few times and soon the dance floor is free and clear of glitter and tears. He makes a large glitter pile to the side of the clearing for the baby Trolls to play in.

'You can get back to dancing,' Branch announces to the rest of the Trolls as his hair bounces back to its usual shape.

DJ Suki starts back up with the beats. The Trolls look so happy to be busting dance moves where they don't slip and slide uncontrollably that their dancing goes to the next level.

Just as Branch finishes his clean up, Poppy, Guy Diamond and Biggie return. They swing into the party with Branch's party supplies, treats and games.

Poppy swings down from the tree next to Branch. 'Where should I put them?' she asks, giving Branch a big smile.

'Anywhere,' Branch replies. 'It's cupcake time!' And with that he takes a cupcake from the tray Poppy is holding and puts the whole thing in his mouth. He smiles at Poppy and cupcake crumbs fall from his mouth.

'Let's eat!' Poppy sings loudly with perfect pitch. The Trolls give another

loud cheer as they try Branch's cupcakes.

'Where should I set these up?' Biggie asks Branch holding up three bright piñatas.

'Anywhere,' Branch replies. 'It's treat time!'

The Trolls give another loud cheer as they line up to have a turn hitting the piñatas. It turns out that Branch has made all three: a Bergen-shaped one, a rainbow shape and a piñata that looks like a cloud.

'Is that safe?' Poppy whispers to Branch who is holding the piñata stick.

'Yes,' Branch replies with a grin. 'The sticks are made from plant stalks so nobody can do too much damage.'

'Where do you want these?' Guy Diamond asks Branch. He's standing next to a bunch of soft, squishy mushrooms.

'Anywhere,' Branch replies. 'It's bounce time!'

All the Trolls help Branch line up the mushrooms so the Trolls can bounce across them. Branch has made this course with the brightest mushrooms he could find. It's totally Troll-tastic!

'Thanks so much, Branch,' Guy Diamond says. 'You totally saved this party. I don't know what we would have done without you. The party would have been a disaster.'

All Branch's friends crowd around and give him a cheer. 'Sorry we weren't so keen on *your* party, Branch,' Biggie says. 'It was just all the rules.'

'No worries, guys,' Branch says. 'Just enjoy THIS party. It was a team effort.'

Branch feels proud of himself.

He did manage to organise some fun things for the party and he knows he's always good in a crisis. Maybe he doesn't need to make so many rules after all.

Poppy gently pulls Branch aside. 'So let me get this straight. You made cupcakes, three piñatas and a bouncy course for the party?' Poppy asks.

'Sure did,' Branch replies. 'I thought they would be fun. I know I had lots of rules. It's hard for me to see how to make things fun AND safe. So I usually just make things safe. But I'm working on the fun part.'

Poppy grins.

'You sure are!' Guy Diamond shouts as he somersaults from the bouncy mushrooms to the piñata to give it a whack with his hair.

'That's not exactly the safe fun I had in mind. But I think the biggest danger is behind us,' Branch says.

'You're full of surprises, Branch,' Poppy says, leaning in to give Branch a friendly nudge.

'I have one more,' Branch replies and he pulls Poppy into a tight hug.

The partying continues well into
the night. It's loud, sparkly and fun.
Branch might be a party trooper
after all.

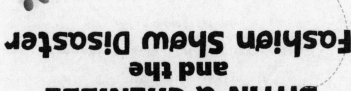

SATIN & CHENILLE and the Fashion Show Disaster

Trolls

DreamWorks

Scholastic Children's Books,
Euston House, 24 Eversholt Street,
London NW1 1DB, UK

A division of Scholastic Ltd
London ~ New York ~ Toronto ~ Sydney ~ Auckland
Mexico City ~ New Delhi ~ Hong Kong

First published in Australia by Bonnier Publishing, 2017, as two titles:
Branch and the Party Rescue
Satin & Chenille and the Makeover Disaster
This edition published in the UK by Scholastic Ltd, 2018

Written by Jaclyn Crupi

ISBN 978 1407 17145 6

Printed and bound in the UK by CPI (Group) Ltd, Croydon, Surrey

2 4 6 8 10 9 7 5 3 1

Papers used by Scholastic Children's Books are made from wood grown in
sustainable forests.

www.scholastic.co.uk

DREAMWORKS

Trolls

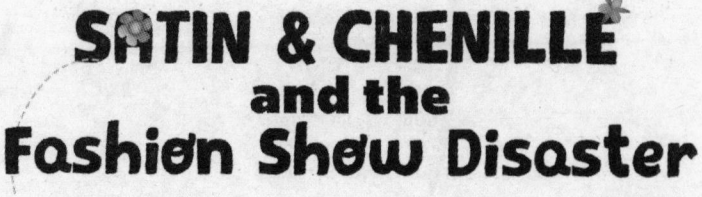

SATIN & CHENILLE
and the
Fashion Show Disaster

SCHOLASTIC

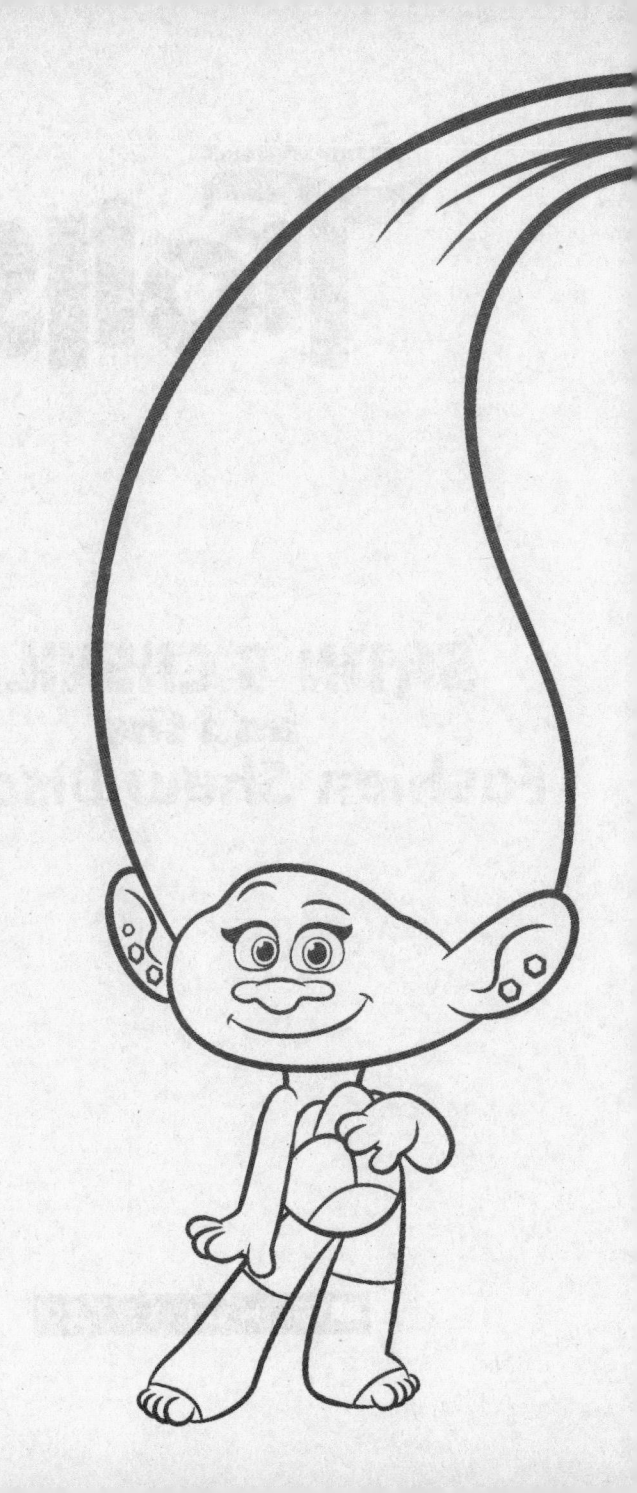

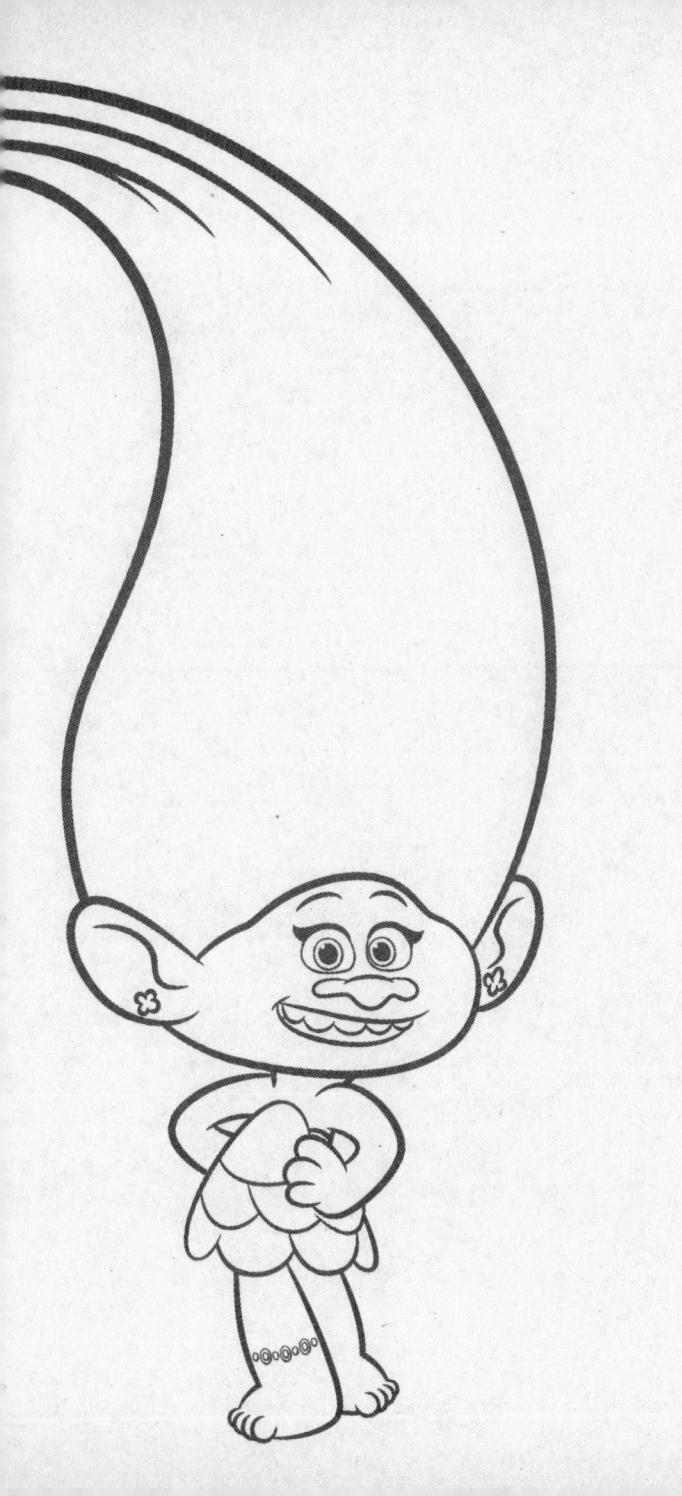

Chapter 1

Satin and Chenille are jumping around their pod with excitement. Their new collection will make an amazing show at Fashion Week!

The fashion-designing twins haven't made the new collection yet. They haven't even started brainstorming ideas. But Satin and Chenille are not worried. They know a stroll around Troll Village will get their creativity flowing. So, with a joyful swing on their hair, the twins zip-line out of their stylish little pod right into Troll Village.

It is a very busy morning. Every Troll is on the go. Troll Village is a blur of bright colours, sparkles and colourful hair.

'You know, Chenille,' Satin says, walking along, 'we don't just need an amazing theme for our new collection. We'll need some help, too. Fashion

Week is only a week away.'

Chenille nods thoughtfully. 'Let's ask our friends to help.'

Satin and Chenille have lots of friends and it's not long before they see one. It's Biggie.

'Oh, Mr Dinkles, you are so cute!' Biggie is saying to his pet worm as his camera goes *snap, snap, snap*.

Satin shouts hello and asks Biggie to help with the fashion show. But Biggie is too busy taking photos of Mr Dinkles in different costumes. The twins chuckle and keep walking.

13

Chenille spots Smidge and waves.
Smidge is busy working out. 'Fifteen,
sixteen...' Smidge counts as she lifts
heavy weights.

'Hey girl! We could use your help—'

'Can't stop,' grunts Smidge,
interrupting Satin. 'Training.'

The twins wave goodbye to their
friend and continue their stroll.
They soon spot DJ Suki and Guy
Diamond.

DJ Suki is busy laying down some
new beats. 'I'm loving this new
mash-up,' she shouts to the twins

over the sound in her headphones.

Satin waves at DJ Suki to remove her headphones so the twins can ask for her help.

'Can't stop,' shouts DJ Suki. 'I'm in the zone!' she grins and keeps bopping.

Guy Diamond is busy dancing up a glitter storm. 'Have a glitter day!' he shouts, grooving past Poppy without stopping.

Poppy, the pink queen of the Trolls, is on a nearby patch of grass scrapbooking. 'Thanks for the sparkles, Guy Diamond,' she calls.

Satin stops short. 'Poppy! Of course,' she says and Chenille nods. 'She's our girl.'

Satin stops short. 'Poppy! Of course,' she says and Chenille nods. 'She's our girl.'

Poppy looks up from her scrapbook. 'Hey Satin, hey Chenille,' she says. 'Guy Diamond just left a glitter trail and I'm loving how it's looking on this scrapbook page. That guy works magic.'

'Girl, we need your help,' Chenille says.

'Okay,' Poppy says, rolling her glue stick over the scrapbook page.

'Fashion Week is only a week away,' Satin explains.

'Er, sounds great,' Poppy says, sprinkling the loose glitter over the wet glue. 'Hmm, I wonder if I should use all this glitter to create a glitter waterslide 3D pop-up...'

Satin and Chenille exchange confused looks. Satin tries again. 'Poppy, can you help us? You see, we'll be busy making the outfits so we need someone to help keep things organized. And you're so good at it.'

'Yep, right,' Poppy says, then frowns at her scrapbook. 'Maybe I could create

some sort of glitter puffer at the top of the slide that sends the glitter down it...'

Chenille frowns. 'Poppy, are you even listening?'

'... Or do I need to use papier mâché?' Poppy looks puzzled.

'POPPY!' Satin shouts to get her friend's attention.

'Whoa ... why all the shouting?' Poppy asks.

'Can you *please* organize our fashion show?' chorus Satin and Chenille.

'Oh, I'd love to,' Poppy says brightly. 'But I am deep in this scrapbooking challenge right now. Can I do it later?'

The twins nod. They can see Poppy is far too busy to help them right now. 'Sure,' says Chenille.

Satin feels a little worried though. 'What are we going to do now?' she asks as the twins walk off.

But Chenille has a plan. 'It's okay,' she says. 'Let's work out the theme for our collection first and get that going. Poppy can help us later.'

'Good plan,' says Satin. 'But what's our theme going to be?' Satin looks around her. 'We need something WOW to kick off Fashion Week.' Chenille looks thoughtful too.

'You said it, girl ... but what?'

Just then, Branch comes around the corner. He is carrying a huge pile of firewood.

'Hi Satin, hi Chenille,' Branch says. 'I'm stockpiling for winter. You never can start too early. Best to be prepared, I say.'

Satin looks at Chenille. Chenille raises her eyebrow. Then they both stare at Branch.

Branch stops in his tracks. 'Guys? Er, are you okay?' Branch asks. 'Why are you looking at me like that?'

'Uh-huh. He really needs our help,' Satin says under her breath.

'You're thinking what I'm thinking?' Chenille asks Satin.

'Mm-hm!' Satin says.

Chapter 2

'Male model!' Satin and Chenille shout at the same time, clapping their hands.

'Say what?' Branch says, dropping the firewood in surprise.

'We're going to make you the star of our fashion show!' the twins exclaim with glee.

'Right … well … hey … um … how do I say this?' Branch strokes his chin thoughtfully. 'NO!' he shouts. Branch starts collecting the dropped firewood.

But Satin and Chenille can't hear Branch over their own excited chatter.

'We'll have to work on outfits obviously, but I think there is a lot we can do with the hair and accessories,' Satin says, touching Branch's hair.

Chenille sticks her face right in close to Branch's to get a better look. 'Hmm … not to mention what a little glam session could do,' she adds.

'Hey, did you guys not hear me? I said no,' Branch says. He continues to pile the wood into his arms. 'A little help here would be nice. Satin, could you add that last log to the top of the pile?'

But the twins don't hear him. They are now in full fashion-show-planning mode. The creative ideas are really starting to flow.

'We will definitely need to include some sparkle and really bright colours,' says Satin.

'Yes, exactly! I mean, I'm thinking sparkles, sparkles, sparkles! We need to make his look really POP,' Chenille says.

A voice breaks into the conversation, snapping Satin and Chenille out of their creative flow. It's Branch. Satin and Chenille had forgotten he was there!

'Look,' Branch is saying. 'I hate to break up your little planning party over here but there is no way I will be in a fashion show. I don't know exactly

what a fashion show is but it doesn't sound like it is for me.'

Satin and Chenille are genuinely shocked and think the same thing. *How can Branch not know what a fashion show is? And how can he not want to be part of it?*

'But we can help you, Branch,' Satin says kindly. 'We'll bring your look to life.'

'I don't have a look,' Branch says, 'And I don't want a look. I like my sensible clothing and functional hair.'

The twins are really confused now.

'But, you can't possibly,' Chenille says. 'We could transform you.'

'That sounds terrible,' Branch says. He is starting to back away from the twins with his pile of firewood.

The sound of singing breaks the silence. *'Glitter pens, stickers, mini pom-poms and yarn, glitter pens ...'*

'Ah, here comes Poppy, let's ask her what she thinks,' says Satin. 'Hey Poppy, we need your opinion over here,' she shouts out.

'Sure guys, what's up?' Poppy says, coming over.

'Don't you think Branch will make the most perfect fashion show model?' Satin asks Poppy.

Satin and Chenille are bursting with excitement as Poppy looks first at each of them and then at Branch, straining under his load of firewood. The fashion duo has a vision and they cannot wait to get to work.

'I would not make the perfect fashion show model,' Branch hisses, 'because I'm not going to be a fashion show model.'

Satin grips Chenille's hand in alarm and Chenille shoots her a worried look.

29

'Hang on now, Branch,' Poppy says. 'Have you ever been in a fashion show?'

'No,' Branch replies.

'Well they're super cool and Satin and Chenille are professionals. They understand fashion. Maybe you should give it a try. You know, be open to new things. Who knows, you might just love it!'

Satin and Chenille smile from ear to ear. They *are* professionals! They know exactly how to change Branch from a regular Troll to a fashion star. Poppy's wise words seem to have a strong effect

on Branch. He puts down his firewood pile and listens. Poppy reminds Branch how great he's been doing at being more positive. Satin and Chenille nod in agreement. Branch has been trying to be open to new things. He has been trying to be less cautious.

The twins and Poppy give Branch big smiles. The twins honestly think that Branch might enjoy being part of their show.

Branch takes a deep breath and closes his eyes for a moment. The twins both hold their breath.

'Okay,' he says quietly. 'I'll be in your fashion show.'

Satin and Chenille smack a high five.

Chapter 3

The twins are so thrilled about
Branch being part of their fashion
show. They race to their pod to get to
work on the new collection. Poppy
and Branch join them.

True to her promise, Poppy finished
her scrapbook project and is helping
the twins get themselves organized.

Branch is sitting quietly in the pod, looking unsure about what is going to happen but still trying to go with the flow.

Satin and Chenille have created a new fashion collection many times. They are total experts. The twins move effortlessly around their colourful pod,

collecting materials and talking through their creative ideas without missing a beat.

'We're going to need a lot of looks,' says Satin as she pulls out a measuring tape.

'We sure are. Patchwork shorts do not work for every occasion,' Chenille says.

'A surfer look?' Satin asks, holding up some fabric samples.

'Yes, perfect,' replies Chenille. 'Board shorts, tousled hair, surfboard.'

'Er, but I can't surf,' Branch pipes up.

'Doesn't matter,' dismisses Satin, waving her hand. 'We'll make you look like you can.'

'Poppy we're going to need you to scrapbook these ideas so we have visual references,' Chenille says, setting up the sewing machine.

'I'm two pages ahead of you,' says Poppy.

The twins spin around to Poppy to see her holding open her scrapbook. The two pages are filled with surfer images and motifs.

'Ooooooohhh! You are good, girl!' coo Satin and Chenille.

'Okay. What other looks?' says Chenille as she grabs Branch's arm and pulls him into the centre of the pod.

'A hipster look,' offers Satin. 'Business casual of course and a preppy look.'

'Does he need a tuxedo do you think?' asks Chenille, spinning Branch around and looking at him from all angles.

'Yes!' Satin and Poppy reply at the same time as Branch shouts no!

'Tell me why I need a tuxedo,' Branch says, rolling his eyes.

'For the after party of course,' says

Satin. 'You'll look great in a tux.'

Chenille swishes past Branch with some fabric samples, accidentally hitting him in the face.

'Okay, so that just leaves hair and make-up,' says Satin.

'Hair and MAKE-UP?' shouts Branch. 'Nobody said anything to me about make-up.'

'Don't worry, Branch,' Satin says. 'It will just be a little. Mostly glitter – just to bring out your blue tones. You'll look amazing! Trust us.'

'As for hair,' says Chenille, 'I think we have a lot of options.' Chenille starts shaping Branch's hair, but he wriggles out of her grasp and sits back down. Chenille doesn't mind. She has plenty more to do. The fashion show is going full steam ahead and there is no stopping it now.

Satin checks on Poppy. She is scrapbooking frantically, trying to get all of the twins' ideas down. Poppy's tongue pokes out as she concentrates hard on cutting, sticking and decorating. 'Nice work, Poppy,' Satin says. 'Okay, what next, Chenille?'

'We need his measurements,' says Chenille.

'I've got it,' says Satin, grabbing the measuring tape. She pulls Branch back to his feet and starts to measure his arms. Satin calls the measurements over to Chenille who writes them down. Satin spins Branch around so she can take all the measurements they

will need to make the outfits.

'I want to try some headbands and hats too, so measure that head of his,' says Chenille.

Satin roughly sweeps Branch's hair out of the way and measures his head.

'Ouch,' says Branch.

'Sorry,' sings Satin. 'Okay I think I have everything.' She returns to the worktop and starts to measure and cut fabric. Chenille is sewing up a storm in no time.

Poppy is still busy trying to capture all the looks they mentioned.

41

As she clips out a piece of rainbow fabric, Satin has an amazing idea. 'Are you thinking what I'm thinking?' she asks her sister.

'I'm thinking jumpsuit,' says Chenille.

'We're thinking jumpsuit!' the twins shout happily.

Poppy cheers and starts to scrapbook jumpsuit ideas. The twins keep having new ideas and adding looks for Poppy to scrapbook.

Branch can only watch on nervously.

Chapter 4

Time always flies when Satin and Chenille are working on a new collection. There is just so much to do! If it were not for Hug Time, the twins would not notice the hours passing by.

They have stopped for Hug Time four times since arriving at the pod. Now, at last, it is time for Satin and Chenille to see all the outfits on Branch and to make any adjustments.

After all their hard work, the fashion twins are so excited to see their creations on their new fashion star.

Chenille knows Branch is new to fashion, so she gives him clear instructions. 'Branch we need you to put on each outfit we have laid out. There are matching accessories for each. Make sure you put those on, too, as they're part of our fashion vision.'

She looks closely at Branch to make sure he has understood.

Branch nods and steps into the fitting room. He comes out wearing the first outfit – a pair of tight white pants with

44

a pink shirt and a blue jumper.

'No, no, no,' Chenille says as Branch emerges. 'The jumper sits *over* your shoulders, tied at the front.' She rearranges the jumper and stands back.

'It's itchy,' Branch says, scratching the back of his neck.

'I like this,' Satin says, pointing at Branch. 'Preppy suits him.'

'Hmm ... the pants are a little loose at the back,' Chenille points out and goes to pin them right as Branch twists.

'OUCH!' Branch cries out, startling Chenille.

'Whoops,' Chenille says as she pulls the pin from his bottom. 'Sorry.'

'Next!' snaps Satin.

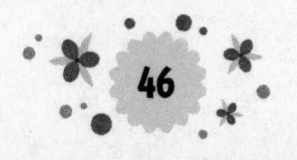

Branch returns to the fitting room and emerges in a tuxedo. Poppy is completely taken aback and puts her hand to her mouth. The twins high five.

'Oh, this look is classic,' says Satin.

'Perfection,' agrees Chenille. 'Definitely our best work yet.'

Branch looks down at his new clothes. When he looks up his face is glum.

Satin and Chenille are alarmed at Branch's sad expression. 'What is it? Did we leave a pin in?' asks Chenille.

'Guys,' Branch says, 'I see you've done a lot of work but this just doesn't feel right ...'

'Where? Too tight around the tummy?' Satin asks, spinning Branch around.

'No, it's not that,' Branch says and sighs. 'It just doesn't feel like me. It's not something I would wear. I'm not comfortable.'

'Oh, Branch, that's where you're wrong,' Chenille says. 'You look wonderful. Don't fall back into your old grumpy ways. Can't you see how good you look?'

Branch frowns at his reflection in the mirror, but Satin jumps in. 'This is a great look on you. It's important to dress for success, Branch.'

'Dress for success?' Branch says quietly. 'I dress for practicality. To me, success is being ready for anything. So I'd say I already dress for success.'

Satin and Chenille shake their heads. *Why can't he see how great he looks right now?* They convince Branch they'll help him see how fun fashion can be and how great he can look at the same time. Branch reluctantly agrees to give it another shot.

As the fitting session goes on, the twins notice Branch is looking more and more unhappy. But Satin and Chenille have a trick up their sleeves! The final outfit. They know when Branch sees himself in it, he will change his mind about the whole collection.

Satin and Chenille proudly present a rainbow-coloured glitter jumpsuit with neon arm warmers. The twins grip each other's hands in excitement as Branch comes out of the fitting room.

Poppy jumps up and claps. 'I love it!' she exclaims. 'It's so bright and shiny and happy.'

'You forgot the rainbow-coloured fedora,' Satin says as she places it atop Branch's head. 'Now, the look is complete.'

'You don't think it's a bit too much?' Branch asks but nobody answers.

Satin and Chenille are busy making small adjustments to Branch's outfit to make it perfect. They pin the jumpsuit at various points. The twins twirl Branch around to look at the outfit from every angle. They don't mean to be rough, but they are so focused they forget that Branch is inside the jumpsuit.

'Okay?' Satin asks stepping back and checking the new fit. She looks up at Branch's face.

For the first time she notices Branch's shoulders hunched and his cheeks a shade of grumpy green. 'NOT okay!' Branch mutters through gritted teeth.

Then, to Satin and Chenille's surprise, their fashion star explodes.

Chapter 5

'I can't do this! It's not me!' Branch shouts. He takes off the fedora and neon arm warmers and storms out of the twins' pod.

Satin and Chenille run to the pod entrance to stop him. But Branch is too fast. They watch on as he swings to the forest floor. Satin notices that he doesn't even stop to collect his firewood from earlier.

She thinks of shouting out to remind him, but stops herself. She doesn't want to make him more angry.

Instead she, Chenille and Poppy watch in silence as Branch stomps through Troll Village and disappears around a corner, still wearing his rainbow jumpsuit.

'He's probably going home,' Poppy says quietly. 'He needs to feel like himself for a while.'

The twins feel shocked.

'What just happened?' Satin asks.

'He looked so good,' says Chenille. 'But he kept saying he was uncomfortable. I just thought he didn't like being the centre of attention.'

'Me too,' says Satin.

'I should have listened to him more,' says Poppy.

'Yeah,' agrees Satin. 'We all should have listened.'

'He may have *looked* good,' says Poppy,

'but I don't think he *felt* good.'

'I think that's what he was saying,' Satin says. 'We weren't listening. I think we all got a little carried away with the outfits and the fashion and we forgot about Branch.'

The twins realize that they have been so focused on the fashion and the outfits and their vision that they have forgotten to think about their friend. Branch is not a tuxedo Troll. He is not a preppy Troll. He is not a surfer Troll. And he is certainly not a rainbow jumpsuit Troll. He is Branch – the most practical and determined Troll in Troll Village. And that's why they love him.

'We tried to change Branch rather than to think about what Branch likes,' Satin says.

'Fashion should never try to change someone but rather help their best self shine through,' Chenille adds.

'I feel terrible about ignoring Branch and forcing him to wear outfits that didn't make him feel good,' says Satin. 'We need to make this right.'

'We will,' says Chenille. 'We just need to put our heads together and come up with a plan.'

'I'll help!' says Poppy.

Chapter 6

Satin and Chenille are feeling really excited and proud. They put their heads together, (which is not hard given they are joined by their hair) and come up with a new collection! The collection is totally inspired by Branch.

It is a range of outdoorsy and rugged outfits for Branch that is fashion forward but most importantly, totally practical!

'I love these outfits,' says Chenille. 'They just scream Branch!'

'They really do,' says Satin. 'It's his usual look but with a fashion twist.'

'I hope he likes them,' the twins chime together.

As the twins are fussing over the clothes and accessories Branch and Poppy come into the pod.

'Thanks so much for coming back, Branch,' Chenille says.

'And thanks for getting him, Poppy,' Satin says.

'I'm sorry I stormed out earlier, but I felt like you weren't listening to me and that made me mad,' says Branch.

'No, we're the ones who are sorry,' says Satin.

'We got carried away with the fashion and the outfits and we forgot to think about you,' adds Chenille. 'We are so sorry.'

'We want to make it up to you, Branch,' says Satin. 'We still want you to star in our fashion show.'

Branch raises his eyebrows. 'I know what you're thinking but ...'

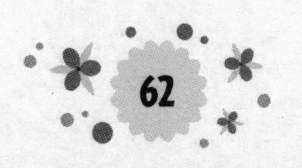

'Poppy has organized it and it's going to be great. We have made you some new outfits that we think you will really like,' says Chenille.

'And if you don't, we'll listen and change them to how you want them to be,' adds Satin.

'The fashion show will be epic,' says Poppy, 'and you don't have to be in it, Branch, if you don't want to. But I think you might have some fun.'

Branch smiles at Poppy. There is a twinkle in her eye.

'Okay sure, let's put on a fashion show,'

Branch agrees.

The twins and Poppy cheer.

'Come and take a look at these outfits,' says Satin. 'We think they are very you.'

Branch goes to the worktop and sees the practical outfits in the browns and greens that are his favourite colours. The twins have obviously put a lot of thought and work into them.

'They're perfect,' Branch says. 'Hang on though, this is a dress,' he adds holding up a brown dress.

'That's for Poppy,' says Chenille. 'We

made matching outfits so you can walk the runway together. We thought that might make it more fun for you, Branch.'

'Yeah, I guess,' says Branch shyly.

To Satin and Chenille's surprise Branch pulls them all into a group hug.

'Wow,' says Satin, 'and it's not even Hug Time!'

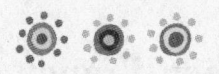

The runway is covered in leaves and branches, the disco balls are shining, DJ Suki is dropping beats and every

Troll is excited for the show to start. But nobody is more excited than Satin and Chenille. Hosting a fashion show to share their new creations with their friends is definitely the best part of being a fashion designer.

The twins step into the spotlight and grab the mic.

'Welcome to our Branch Out fashion show for Fashion Week,' says Satin. The Trolls cheer.

'We have a completely new collection to show you,' says Chenille. 'It's different to anything we have ever done and we're very proud of it.'

'It's fashion that's completely practical and wearable and comfortable,' says Satin.

'We call it ... Branch-wear,' the twins say.

The twins step away to the side and Branch and Poppy take their place. They are at the start of the runway. Poppy and Branch are wearing matching outfits. They look great.

'You ready?' Satin whispers to Branch.

'Sure am,' says Branch. Then he stage-whispers to Satin and Chenille. 'And I feel great!'

He stretches his hand out towards
Poppy, she takes it and they head down
the runway.

Satin and Chenille press their heads
together and squeal. They did it! They
put on their most unique – and maybe
most memorable – fashion show yet
because it showcased the true colours
of a very special friend.

Flip me over for the next story!

Hug Time!

Flip me over for the next story!